LOVE, SIMON
解讀攻略

戴逸群 —— 主編

林冠瑋 —— 編著

Ian Fletcher —— 審閱

三民書局

國家圖書館出版品預行編目資料

Love, Simon 解讀攻略／戴逸群主編；林冠瑋編著.——
初版一刷.——臺北市：三民，2020
面；　公分.——（閱讀成癮）

ISBN 978–957–14–6807–5 （平裝）
1. 英語 2. 讀本

805.18　　　　　　　　　　　　　　109004845

閱讀成癮

Love, Simon 解讀攻略

主　　　編	戴逸群
編 著 者	林冠瑋
審　　　閱	Ian Fletcher
責 任 編 輯	林雅淯
美 術 編 輯	陳奕臻
封 面 繪 圖	Steph Pai

發 行 人	劉振強
出 版 者	三民書局股份有限公司
地　　　址	臺北市復興北路 386 號 (復北門市)
	臺北市重慶南路一段 61 號 (重南門市)
電　　　話	(02)25006600
網　　　址	三民網路書店 https://www.sanmin.com.tw

出 版 日 期	初版一刷 2020 年 5 月
書 籍 編 號	S870480
I S B N	978-957-14-6807-5

三民書局

—— 序 ——

　　新課綱強調以「學生」為中心的教與學，注重學生的學習動機與熱情。而英文科首重語言溝通、互動的功能性，培養學生「自主學習」與「終身學習」的能力與習慣。小說「解讀攻略」就是因應新課綱的精神，在「英文小說中毒團隊」的努力下孕育而生。

　　一系列的「解讀攻略」旨在引導學生能透過原文小說的閱讀學習獨立思考，運用所學的知識與技能解決問題；此外也藉由廣泛閱讀進行跨文化反思，提升社會參與並培養國際觀。

　　「英文小說中毒團隊」由普高技高英文老師與大學教授組成，嚴選出主題多樣豐富、適合英文學習的原文小說。我們從文本延伸，設計多元有趣的閱讀素養活動，培養學生從讀懂文本到表達所思的英文能力。團隊秉持著改變臺灣英文教育的使命感，期許我們的努力能為臺灣的英文教育注入一股活水，翻轉大家對英文學習的想像！

戴逸群

Contents

Picture Credits

All pictures in this publication are authorized for use by Shutterstock.

Chapters 1–2
Pages 1–16

Word Power

1. blackmail *v.* 勒索
2. dumbfounded *adj.* 嚇得目瞪口呆的
3. anecdote *n.* 趣聞軼事
4. pantomime *n.* 默劇

5. blind spot *n.* 盲點
6. matchmaker *n.* 媒人
7. equilibrium *n.* 平衡
8. puberty *n.* 青春期

Reading Comprehension

(　) 1. After reading Simon's emails, what does Martin Addison blackmail Simon into doing?
    (A) Telling him who Blue is.
    (B) Coming out as gay.
    (C) Being his friend.
    (D) Helping him talk to Abby.

(　) 2. Why did Simon use the library computer to check his email?
    (A) Because his laptop was not functioning properly.
    (B) Because he forgot to bring his phone with him to school.
    (C) Because he couldn't wait to check his important email.
    (D) Because he had to search for some information in the library.

(　) 3. Which of the following statements is true about Simon?
    (A) He has dated one boyfriend before.
    (B) He was heartbroken after breaking up with his ex.
    (C) He is a freshman in Creekwood High School.
    (D) He has a secret identity as Jacques.

1. Why did Simon date girls after he knew he was gay? What do you think of this?

_____

_____

_____

_____

_____

_____

2. Imagine you were in Simon's shoes, what would you do if your secret was discovered by Martin Addison?

_____

_____

_____

_____

_____

_____

3. Search the Internet and find out what each letter in "LGBTQ" stands for. How does Simon identify himself?

_____

_____

_____

_____

_____

_____

Character Log

Find each character's basic information, physical appearance, or personality traits from chapter 1 to chapter 10 of the novel and draw a picture of each character.

Simon
- being blackmailed
- gay
- in the drama club
- secret identity: Jacques

Blue

Martin

Leah

Abby

Nick

Bram

Cal

Nora

4

Chapters 3-4
Pages 17-38

Word Power

1. anonymous *adj.* 匿名的
2. disheveled *adj.* (頭髮、服裝) 不整的
3. preoccupied *adj.* 出神的
4. take sth with a grain of salt 對⋯半信半疑
5. objective *n.* 目的
6. intimidate *v.* 恐嚇
7. segregate *v.* 實行種族隔離
8. deliberate *adj.* 故意的

Reading Comprehension

(　) 1. Which of the following statements about Creeksecrets is **NOT** true?
　　(A) It's where you can post anonymous confessions.
　　(B) It's where you can find secret random thoughts.
　　(C) It's where you can comment on anything.
　　(D) It's where you will get judged all the time.

(　) 2. Why does Simon feel worried about Blue finding out Martin has taken a screenshot of their emails?
　　(A) Because Simon does not want to lose contact with Blue.
　　(B) Because Simon is not ready to tell Blue who he is.
　　(C) Because Blue wrote bad stuff about Simon's friends in their emails.
　　(D) Because Simon revealed Blue's identity in the emails.

(　) 3. Since what age have Simon and Nick known each other?
　　(A) Since the age of three.
　　(B) Since the age of six.
　　(C) Since the age of four.
　　(D) Since the age of nine.

1. On page 20, Simon mentions the difference between being gay in New York and in Georgia. In your opinion, would it be more difficult for Simon to be gay in Georgia?

_____

_____

_____

_____

_____

_____

2. On page 33, Simon says "Atlanta is so weirdly segregated, and no one ever talks about it." Why does Simon say that? What do you think he means?

_____

_____

_____

_____

_____

_____

3. Why do you think Simon has been "feeling a little strange" about the girlfriend thing after Blue asked about it?

_____

_____

_____

_____

_____

_____

Letter Writing

Imagine yourself as Jacques and write an email to Blue to tell him about Martin's screenshot of their emails. Try to find the details from the book and use the words which Simon might say.

New Message	_ ⤫ ✕
To	Cc Bcc
Subject	

Send

Chapters 5-6
Pages 39-62

Word Power

1. intertwine *v.* 使纏結

2. self-conscious *adj.* 侷促不安的；自覺的

3. assertive *adj.* 堅定自信的；果敢的

4. astonishingly *adv.* 令人驚訝地

5. miscellaneous *adj.* 各樣的

6. savor *v.* 享用

7. electrified *adj.* 興奮的

8. outright *adv.* 無保留地

Reading Comprehension

(   ) 1. What breed of dog is Bieber?

    (A) Chihuahua.

    (B) Golden Retriever.

    (C) Labrador.

    (D) Bulldog.

(   ) 2. Why does Simon's mom stay up late to wait for Simon and Abby?

    (A) To make sure Simon and Abby come home safely.

    (B) To prepare snacks for Simon and Abby.

    (C) To show her acceptance of partying.

    (D) To scold Simon for being late.

(   ) 3. Why does Simon think his family would be fine with his sexual identity?

    (A) Because his family are religious.

    (B) Because his parents are not Democrats.

    (C) Because his family already know about it.

    (D) Because his family are easy-going. His dad likes to joke around.

Further Discussion

1. Why does Simon feel "strange" at the party?

_____

_____

_____

_____

_____

_____

2. On page 56, Simon says he is "tired of coming out." What does he mean? Do you think it is possible for someone "not to change"?

_____

_____

_____

_____

_____

_____

3. Why does Blue feel so nervous and uncomfortable when Simon asks about how he will dress up?

_____

_____

_____

_____

_____

_____

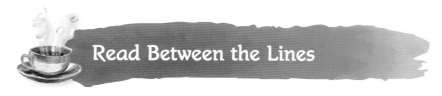

On page 48, Simon says there is an invisible line. On one side of the line are people like Garrett, Abby, and Nick. On the other side are people like Leah, Simon, and Blue. What's your opinion on these two sides?

	People like: _____	People like: _____
Simon's Opinion	• people who go to parties and drink and don't get wasted off of one beer • people who have had sex and don't think it's a huge deal	• people who feel strange or uncomfortable at parties • people who have never kissed anyone
Your Opinion		

Chapters 7-8
Pages 63-79

Word Power

1. subversive *adj.* 有顛覆性的
2. reconcile *v.* 調和；調解
3. mortifying *adj.* 使人難為情的
4. obscene *adj.* 粗俗的；傷風敗俗的

5. mascot *n.* 吉祥物
6. reflex *n.* 本能反應
7. connoisseur *n.* 鑑賞家；行家
8. fantasize *v.* 幻想

Reading Comprehension

(　) 1. Which of the following statements is true about Gender Bender Day?
    (A) Simon loves Gender Bender Day because he can truly be himself.
    (B) All students will dress in cheerleading uniforms on that day.
    (C) Nora dressed up as a trash can on Gender Bender Day.
    (D) People cross-dress on Gender Bender Day.

(　) 2. Which of the following statements is true about Bram Greenfeld?
    (A) He is from the cheerleading team.
    (B) He is a very talkative person.
    (C) He usually eats dinner with Simon.
    (D) He is kind of adorable to Simon.

(　) 3. Why does Leah get angry at Nick?
    (A) Because Nick sits right beside Abby.
    (B) Because Nick keeps staring at Abby.
    (C) Because Nick proposes to go to the football game.
    (D) Because Nick forgets their date at Waffle House.

Further Discussion

1. What is Simon's opinion about masculinity? Why? Do you agree with him?

_____

_____

_____

_____

_____

_____

2. How does Simon feel about cross-dressing?

_____

_____

_____

_____

_____

_____

3. If you were Simon, during the football game, would you test Cal to see if he was Blue? Why or why not?

_____

_____

_____

_____

_____

_____

What's Your Costume?

In chapter 7, people cross-dress for Gender Bender Day. Please write down how the following characters dress for this occasion and imagine what you would wear. Describe your costume and draw it.

Characters	Costume
Simon	
Nick, Garrett, and Bram	
Abby	
Leah	
Martin	

Your Costume
I was born a boy / a girl. For Gender Bender Day, I would . . .

Chapters 9-10
Pages 80-90

Word Power

1. jittery *adj.* 緊張不安的；顫抖的
2. intercept *v.* 攔截
3. ditch *v.* 拋棄
4. leftovers *n.* 吃剩的食物

5. discernible *adj.* 可辨別出的
6. wreckage *n.* 殘骸
7. coherent *adj.* 有條理的
8. warp *v.* 扭曲

Reading Comprehension

(　) 1. Which of the following is most likely to be Garrett's hat?

(A)

(B)

(C)

(D)

(　) 2. Why does Abby make a golden bow tie for Simon?

(A) To tell Simon that she likes him.

(B) To celebrate Simon's golden birthday.

(C) To show her artistic talent to Simon.

(D) To make sure Simon looks nice.

(　) 3. Which of the following is true about Simon's birthday?

(A) It is Simon's eighteenth birthday party.

(B) The flavor of Simon's birthday cake is vanilla.

(C) Everyone should wear a party hat to get a cake.

(D) Simon also invites Cal Price to his party.

1. When Cal Price fails to get the hint of the Oreos, Simon says, "that doesn't have to mean anything." Why does Simon say so?

_____

_____

_____

_____

_____

_____

2. What do Simon and Blue talk about in their emails? Over the past ten chapters, have you found out any differences in the way they write to each other or any chemistry between them?

_____

_____

_____

_____

_____

_____

3. What's your opinion about making friends through the Internet (e.g. through blogs, emails, apps, etc.)? Do you have any personal experience of this?

_____

_____

_____

_____

_____

Creeksecrets is a place where people can post anonymous confessions and secret random thoughts. Here is an anonymous post from Creeksecrets. Please think of two characters' replies with their usernames and your own.

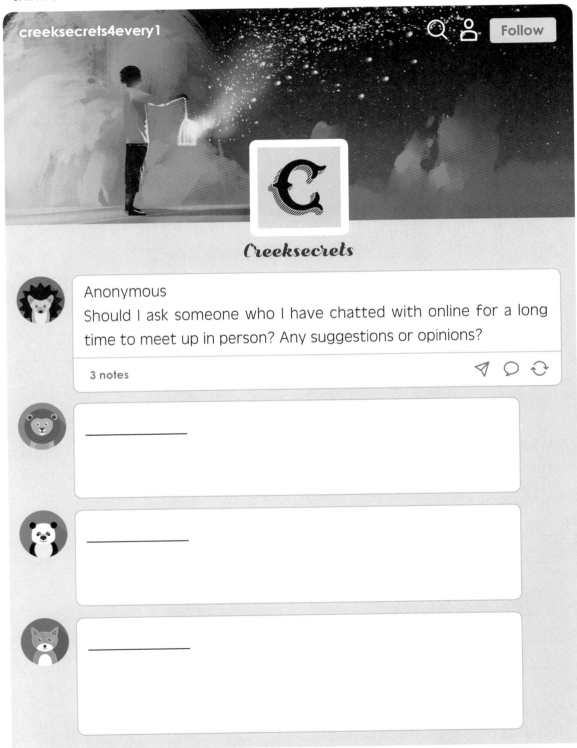

creeksecrets4every1 🔍 👤 Follow

Creeksecrets

Anonymous
Should I ask someone who I have chatted with online for a long time to meet up in person? Any suggestions or opinions?

3 notes

_____

_____

_____

Chapters 11-12
Pages 91-107

Word Power

1. villainous *adj.* 邪惡的
2. burrow *v.* 鑽進
3. hardcore *adj.* 信念堅定的
4. stink-eye *n.* 不悅表情
5. nosy *adj.* 好管閒事的

6. paranoid *adj.* 多疑的
7. intangible *adj.* 難以形容的
8. hipster *n.* 趕時髦的人
9. matrilineal *adj.* 母系的

Reading Comprehension

(　) 1. Why is Nick Eisner's name used for peanut butter cookies?
(A) Because Nick loves eating peanut butter cookies.
(B) Because Nick is disgusted by peanut butter cookies.
(C) Because Nick once misunderstood what peanut butter cookies were.
(D) Because Nick had peanut butter for breakfast when he was five.

(　) 2. In Simon's opinion, why does Martin stand up for Abby when Simon calls her a bitch?
(A) He tries to look good in front of Abby.
(B) He is a decent and nice guy.
(C) He hates seeing classmates being bullied.
(D) He wants to impress Simon.

(　) 3. To which family member does Blue plan to come out to first?
(A) His mother.
(B) His father.
(C) His stepmother.
(D) His sibling.

Further Discussion

1. What's your opinion about Martin standing up for Abby when Simon called her a bitch? If you were Abby, how would you feel?

   _____
   _____
   _____
   _____
   _____
   _____

2. How does Simon feel when he finds Leah and Nick hang out without him? Why do you think he feels this way?

   _____
   _____
   _____
   _____
   _____
   _____

3. Blue mentions that there are two kinds of parents when their own kid comes out. What are they? Do you agree with him?

   _____
   _____
   _____
   _____
   _____
   _____

On page 99, Simon says that his name Simon means "the one who hears," and Spier means "the one who watches." Is there any meaning behind your name? Please complete the table below.

	First name	Last name
Who gave you the name?		
Meanings behind your name		

Chapters 13-14
Pages 108-119

Word Power

1. twisty *adj.* 彎彎曲曲的
2. obsessed *adj.* 著迷的
3. blasphemous *adj.* 褻瀆的
4. maneuver *n.* 巧妙動作；花招

5. prominent *adj.* 突出的，顯眼的
6. photographic memory *n.* 準確的記憶力
7. metabolism *n.* 新陳代謝
8. surreal *adj.* 離奇的；超現實的

Reading Comprehension

(　) 1. Why does Simon invite Abby and Martin to Waffle House?
   (A) Because he wants to hang out with them.
   (B) Because he is forced to create opportunities for Martin to be with Abby.
   (C) Because he cannot find any other friend to go with him.
   (D) Because he wants to practice his lines.

(　) 2. How does Blue realize that his father has no idea he is gay?
   (A) By seeing the interaction between his divorced parents.
   (B) By listening to his father's opinions about gay people.
   (C) By reading his father's book about Oscar Wilde.
   (D) By receiving Casanova's book from his father.

(　) 3. In the end, why does Blue decide to tell his mom first rather than his dad?
   (A) Because telling his dad first might hurt his mom's feelings.
   (B) Because telling his mom first might be much easier.
   (C) Because his mom has already figured it out.
   (D) Because his dad shows little interest in listening to him.

Further Discussion

1. What is Martin's motive for introducing his brother to Simon?

_____

_____

_____

_____

_____

_____

2. What's the difference between Casanova and Oscar Wilde? Is there any hint from the text?

_____

_____

_____

_____

_____

_____

3. If you were to tell someone your big hidden secret, what would you be worried about? On the other hand, what would you do if you were told a secret by someone else?

_____

_____

_____

_____

_____

Let's do a character analysis of Martin Addison. Complete the table below to understand more about Martin.

What does Martin look like?	Describe the relationship between Martin, Abby, and Simon.
What does Martin do during the break of history class?	**Describe how Martin behaves in Waffle House.**

Chapters 15-16
Pages 120-129

Word Power

1. sleepover *n.* 留宿
2. slog *v.* 艱難地行走
3. fling *v.* (肢體) 猛地一動
4. gape *v.* 目瞪口呆地看

5. stunned *adj.* 震驚的
6. amped *adj.* 興奮的
7. analytical *adj.* 分析的
8. momentous *adj.* 重大的

Reading Comprehension

( ) 1. Where does Abby stay for the night after practice?
   (A) She goes back home because the next day is a school day.
   (B) She goes back home because she can't sleep over at someone's house.
   (C) She stays at Simon's place because she doesn't have a car that night.
   (D) She stays at Simon's place because the bus will not be running that night.

( ) 2. What does Martin do that makes Abby and Simon feel stunned and awkward at the WaHo?
   (A) He speaks loudly when practicing lines.
   (B) He dances like a monkey in the booth.
   (C) He sings the entire song with his Fagin voice.
   (D) He shows his love to Abby in front of everyone.

( ) 3. How does Abby feel after Simon comes out to her?
   (A) She shows little interest in it.
   (B) She is very surprised at the secret.
   (C) She is not ready to face the truth.
   (D) She is honored to be the first one to know.

1. How does Abby react to Martin's embarrassing behavior at the WaHo? If you were Abby, what would you do?

_____

_____

_____

_____

_____

_____

2. How does Abby react when Simon comes out to her? Answer with descriptions of her body language or her words.

_____

_____

_____

_____

_____

_____

3. How do Blue and Simon describe their feelings and experiences about coming out?

_____

_____

_____

_____

_____

_____

Simon's Emotional Range

In these two chapters, Simon's emotions go up and down with different events. Please write down how Simon feels about each event with textual evidence and draw the emotional range.

Events	Simon's Feelings
Abby's sleepover	Simon loves their sleepovers.
Practicing at the WaHo	
Coming out to Abby	
Before going home	
Writing to Blue	

Chapters 17-18
Pages 130-149

Word Power

1. restless *adj.* 坐立難安的

2. debilitate *v.* 使身心衰弱

3. insurmountable *adj.* 難以克服的

4. triumphant *adj.* 洋洋得意的

5. thud *v.* 砰砰地跳

6. bewildered *adj.* 感到困惑的

7. excruciating *adj.* 極尷尬的

8. tangential *adj.* 不相關的

Reading Comprehension

( ) 1. Why does Simon have trouble focusing in school?

(A) Because he is thinking about the sophomore that snuck into the lab.

(B) Because he has been rehearsing late at the WaHo these days.

(C) Because he is obsessed and a bit in love with Blue.

(D) Because he is worried about coming out to Leah and Nick.

( ) 2. Which of the following is **NOT** true about Simon when he thinks about coming out to Leah and Nick?

(A) Coming out to Leah and Nick is much easier than to Abby.

(B) Simon worries whether Leah and Nick could still recognize him.

(C) Simon feels relieved when receiving a call from his dad.

(D) Sharing their crushes is never a topic in their conversations.

( ) 3. Why did Blue fail to come out to his dad?

(A) Because Blue can't make up his mind.

(B) Because Blue can't find the opportunity.

(C) Because Blue's mom doesn't want him to do so.

(D) Because Blue enjoys listening to his father.

1. What does Simon think about coming out to Leah and Nick?

   _____

   _____

   _____

   _____

   _____

   _____

2. What is the thing that Simon and Blue point out as default in chapter 18? Do you agree with their idea?

   _____

   _____

   _____

   _____

   _____

   _____

3. On page 145, Simon mentions that the equivalent of coming out for a straight person is knocking someone up. In your opinion, is there anything else people do that counts as "coming out" to some degree?

   _____

   _____

   _____

   _____

   _____

   _____

Relationship Detective

In chapter 17, Simon's interactions with other characters are described in detail. Imagine you are a detective, please find textual evidence of each interaction (A–C) and write down your interpretation.

(A) Cal pushes Simon on a rolling chair down the hall.

(C) Martin is mad at Simon.

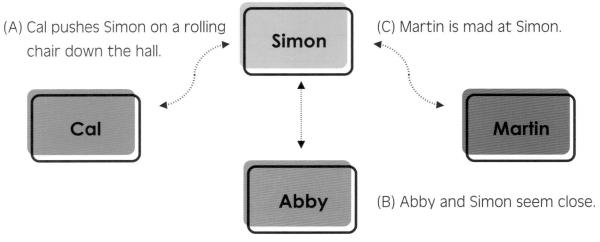

(B) Abby and Simon seem close.

	Textual Evidence	My Interpretation
(A)		
(B)		
(C)		

Chapters 19-20
Pages 150-171

Word Power

1. scavenger hunt *n.* 尋寶
2. newsfeed *n.* 動態消息
3. realm *n.* 領域，範圍
4. common denominator *n.* 共同點

5. tidings *n.* 消息
6. avalanche *n.* 大量
7. mope *v.* 悶悶不樂
8. elaborate *v.* 詳細說明

Reading Comprehension

( ) 1. Why do Leah and Nick ask Simon if he wants to talk?
(A) Because they know about something but dare not ask directly.
(B) Because they have decided to date and become a couple.
(C) Because Leah wants to admit that she likes Nick.
(D) Because Leah worries that she might lose Simon as a friend.

( ) 2. Who tells Simon about the post that reveals his sexual identity on the Tumblr?
(A) Alice.
(B) Leah.
(C) Nick.
(D) Nora.

( ) 3. Why doesn't Alice share the news that she has a boyfriend with her family?
(A) Because she is not satisfied with her boyfriend.
(B) Because she knows they will ask many questions and even stalk him online.
(C) Because she doesn't think her family will like him.
(D) Because she and her boyfriend only talk online and have never met in person.

Further Discussion

1. Why do Leah and Nick go to Simon's place? If you were in their situation, what would you do?

_____

_____

_____

_____

_____

_____

2. After Simon tells his family about his sexual identity, his father asks him who turned him off women. What do you think about his father's words?

_____

_____

_____

_____

_____

_____

3. If you dated someone, would you share the news with your family members? Why or why not?

_____

_____

_____

_____

_____

_____

Simon's Playlist

In chapter 19, Simon mentions his sad playlist "The Great Depression." Please think about what other songs you would recommend Simon to add to the playlist and share your favorite lines and feelings about the songs.

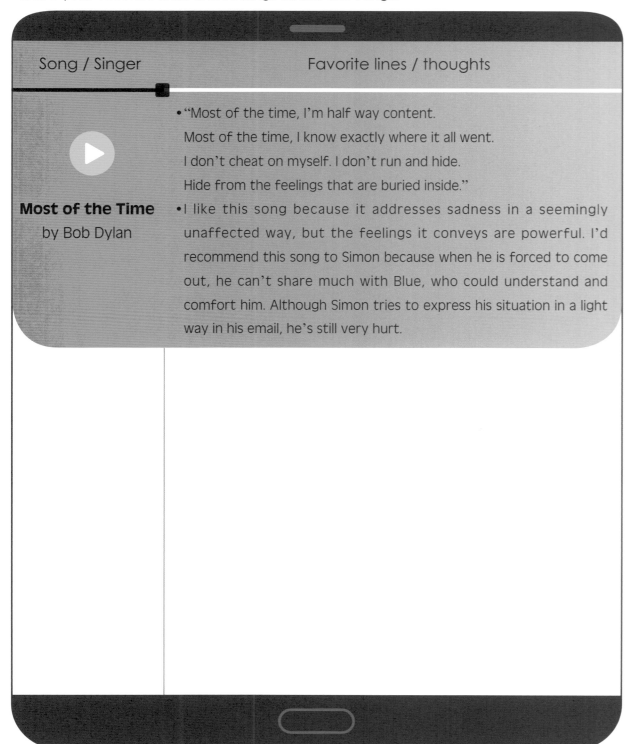

Song / Singer	Favorite lines / thoughts
Most of the Time by Bob Dylan	• "Most of the time, I'm half way content. Most of the time, I know exactly where it all went. I don't cheat on myself. I don't run and hide. Hide from the feelings that are buried inside." • I like this song because it addresses sadness in a seemingly unaffected way, but the feelings it conveys are powerful. I'd recommend this song to Simon because when he is forced to come out, he can't share much with Blue, who could understand and comfort him. Although Simon tries to express his situation in a light way in his email, he's still very hurt.

Song / Singer	Favorite lines / thoughts

Chapters 21–22
Pages 172–185

Word Power

1. lanky *adj.* 高瘦的
2. blast *v.* 發出巨響
3. startle *v.* 使大吃一驚
4. presentable *adj.* 體面的

5. overstimulated *adj.* 過度興奮的
6. radiate *v.* 散發；流露
7. grimace *v.* 做鬼臉
8. disoriented *adj.* 迷失的

Reading Comprehension

( ) 1. Who is Carter Addison?
    (A) Simon's ex-boyfriend.
    (B) Simon's teacher.
    (C) Martin's brother.
    (D) Martin's friend.

( ) 2. Why does Alice become annoyed outside the Waffle House?
    (A) Because Simon doesn't talk to her.
    (B) Because Simon and Nora both suddenly run off.
    (C) Because Alice forgets to bring money with her.
    (D) Because Nora stands up to her.

( ) 3. What is Nick's reaction when Simon comes out to his friends?
    (A) He takes it calmly.
    (B) He gives Simon a big hug.
    (C) He refuses to believe.
    (D) He is shocked and speechless.

Further Discussion

1. How does Blue feel about Simon's suggestion about exchanging numbers? What are his feelings toward Simon?

_____

_____

_____

_____

_____

_____

2. How does Leah react and feel when she knows that Simon came out to Abby first? If you were Leah, would you get mad at Simon?

_____

_____

_____

_____

_____

_____

3. How much do you think Nora has changed? How?

_____

_____

_____

_____

_____

_____

Character Word Cloud

Who is your favorite character? Come up with at least ten words related to this character, whether they are about their character traits, personality, family background, interests, or appearance. Then, create a word cloud portraying this character, or you may include a picture, image, or symbol that you think can represent him/her.

My favorite character is:

◇◇

Words	Textual Evidence

12

Chapters 23–24
Pages 186–202

Word Power

1. atrium *n.* 中庭，天井
2. homophobic *adj.* 恐同的
3. irreparably *adv.* 無可挽救地
4. commotion *n.* 騷動；混亂

5. calf *n.* 小腿肌
6. ogle *v.* 色瞇瞇地看
7. therapeutic *adj.* 有療效的
8. obscure *adj.* 鮮為人知的

Reading Comprehension

(　　) 1. Who is the person that Simon encourages to be braver and ask Leah out for a date?
    (A) Garrett.
    (B) Bram.
    (C) Nick.
    (D) Cal.

(　　) 2. Why does the rehearsal get interrupted?
    (A) Because Martin forgets his lines during the rehearsal.
    (B) Because there are two dudes holding giant poster board signs.
    (C) Because Abby sees her friends in the auditorium.
    (D) Because Ms. Albright is not satisfied with the rehearsal.

(　　) 3. Why does Martin wait for Simon by his car?
    (A) To laugh at Simon's miserable day.
    (B) To delete the screenshots in person.
    (C) To have a ride home together.
    (D) To apologize for what he has done.

1. When students make fun of Simon during the rehearsal, how does Ms. Albright feel? Is there any policy enforced in your school to stop bullying?

_____

_____

_____

_____

_____

_____

2. What does Simon accuse Martin of? Which character do you have sympathy for and why?

_____

_____

_____

_____

_____

_____

3. Simon mentions that he didn't expect Garrett and Bram to be cool about him being gay. Why would he have that impression? What is your opinion?

_____

_____

_____

_____

_____

_____

Gender Stereotypes

Do all girls love pink? Don't boys cry? Gender stereotypes are beliefs that use certain characteristics to define what females and males can do, generally based on gender. Please write down some examples of gender stereotypes you've encountered or heard of. Then, share your reflections below.

Why don't you put on some make-up? All girls do!

What do you mean you don't want kids?

You should try to lose some weight.

I thought girls aren't good at math!

You're too thin for a boy. You should work out.

Come on! Don't be so gay.

Why are you crying? Real men don't cry.

Fashion is a girl thing. Man up!

What do you think about gender stereotypes? Do you conform to them or challenge them?

Chapters 25-27
Pages 203-221

Word Power

1. penetrate *v.* 進入；穿透

2. quell *v.* 平息；制止

3. perch *v.* 棲息於

4. smug *adj.* 沾沾自喜的

5. listless *adj.* 懶散的，無精打采的

6. seismic *adj.* 重大的，劇烈的

7. adrenaline *n.* 腎上腺素

8. incredulously *adv.* 不能相信地

Reading Comprehension

(　) 1. What does "*Jacques a dit*" mean?

    (A) Simon says.

    (B) Simon sings.

    (C) Simon dances.

    (D) Simon laughs.

(　) 2. Why does Ms. Albright ask Simon out for a minute before the show?

    (A) To encourage Simon to enjoy their second show.

    (B) To ask Simon whether he is under the weather or not.

    (C) To tell Simon someone altered the cast list.

    (D) To share good news about the bullies being punished.

(　) 3. What does Ms. Albright do before the second performance starts?

    (A) She scolds those who laugh at Simon.

    (B) She reviews the zero tolerance policy with the audience.

    (C) She introduces the show and welcomes everyone.

    (D) She invites Simon to say something on the stage.

1. What does Simon find in the plastic bag? What do you think this mean?

   _____

   _____

   _____

   _____

   _____

   _____

2. What is Simon's realization after he fails to figure out who Blue is? Have you
   ever experienced the same feelings?

   _____

   _____

   _____

   _____

   _____

   _____

3. If you were Simon, would you cancel the show because people altered the
   names of the cast? Why or why not?

   _____

   _____

   _____

   _____

   _____

   _____

Think OREO

We all know that Simon loves eating Oreos. However, do you know that OREO is also a good strategy to help organize opinions? Try to use this strategy to express your opinions about the cast list being altered.

Opinion Write a topic sentence to share your opinion.

Reason Give reason(s) to explain why you think that way.

Example Give examples and details.

Opinion Restate your opinion.

42

Chapter 28
Pages 222–239

Word Power

1. unfathomable *adj.* 難以理解的
2. deflate *v.* 使洩氣
3. contagious *adj.* 有感染力的
4. paperback *n.* 平裝書

5. merge *v.* 併入
6. briskly *adv.* 輕快地
7. pine for sb/sth 思念⋯
8. upholstery *n.* 座位表面材料

Reading Comprehension

( ) 1. Why is Leah not invited to the trip after the show?
    (A) Because Leah is angry with Simon.
    (B) Because Leah is busy with school work.
    (C) Because Leah hates Abby.
    (D) Because Leah is sometimes moody.

( ) 2. Which of the following statements is **NOT** true about Peter?
    (A) He has extremely white teeth.
    (B) He has brown hair.
    (C) He studies at Emory.
    (D) He is a junior.

( ) 3. What do Simon's parents do after finding out he is drunk?
    (A) They say they are fine with Simon drinking alcohol.
    (B) They decide to ground Simon for two days.
    (C) They take away Simon's phone immediately.
    (D) They scold Abby and Nick for taking Simon out.

Further Discussion

1. Simon says Alice and Nora are terrible. Why? What do you think of Simon for saying that?

_____

_____

_____

_____

_____

_____

2. In Webster's, after finding out Simon is only a high school student, Peter says "Go be seventeen." What is your interpretation of this statement? What is special about being seventeen?

_____

_____

_____

_____

_____

_____

3. What strikes Simon as unusual when he confronts his father? What does Simon call his father out on?

_____

_____

_____

_____

_____

_____

What Will Your Life Be Like?

What was your life at seventeen like? If you're not yet seventeen, what will it be like? Was/Is it full of books and tests, or school clubs and self-exploration? Please also write down your expectations for your future at the ages of twenty-seven and thirty-seven.

Chapters 29-30
Pages 240-256

Word Power

1. pry *v.* 打聽
2. earshot *n.* 聽力範圍
3. custody *n.* 拘留
4. sarcastic *adj.* 諷刺的
5. rein sth in 約束；制止
6. self-contained *adj.* 獨立的
7. earnest *adj.* 誠摯的
8. crotchety *adj.* 易怒的

Reading Comprehension

( ) 1. What happened to Nick and Abby after Friday night?
    (A) They had a serious quarrel.
    (B) They decided to date.
    (C) They apologized to Leah for not inviting her.
    (D) They got Simon a boyfriend in school.

( ) 2. Why is Leah so sad and mean when seeing Simon?
    (A) Because Nick and Abby have become a couple.
    (B) Because Simon came out to Nick first.
    (C) Because she was not invited to hang out.
    (D) Because she didn't get an invitation to the show.

( ) 3. How can Simon be sure that Martin is not Blue?
    (A) Simon confronts Martin and asks him about it.
    (B) Martin is not half-Jewish.
    (C) Simon used to get emails while rehearsing.
    (D) Martin doesn't share a name with a president.

1. When Simon finally gets to talk to Leah, how does their conversation go? Does she really mean what she says?

_____

_____

_____

_____

_____

_____

2. On page 249, Simon's mom says that she used to see every tiny change in her kids, but now, she is missing out. What do you think of her words?

_____

_____

_____

_____

_____

_____

3. If you were Abby, how would you feel about being manipulated or forced to like someone you didn't like?

_____

_____

_____

_____

_____

_____

Old Way, New Way

Simon's mom says that she used to be able to see every tiny change in her kids. However, now, she is missing stuff. Please think about how much you have changed and interview your parents to find out their attitude to those changes.

I used to . . .	Now I . . .	My Parents think . . .

Chapters 31-32
Pages 257-270

Word Power

1. shoulder blade *n.* 肩胛骨
2. postscript *n.* (信末的) 補充
3. perpetual *adj.* 永久的
4. haywire *adj.* 失去控制的

5. monumental *adj.* 極度的
6. taut *adj.* 拉緊的
7. clockwise *adj.* 順時針的
8. eerie *adj.* 怪異的

Reading Comprehension

( ) 1. What is the purpose of Simon's email in chapter 31?

    (A) To show that he is tired of guessing who Blue really is.

    (B) To express his sadness about Blue's rejection.

    (C) To confess his feelings for Blue and invite him to meet.

    (D) To disclose his real identity so Blue can find him.

( ) 2. What does Simon find inside the T-shirt?

    (A) A note from Blue to him.

    (B) A poem about Blue's feelings for him.

    (C) A ticket to Elliott Smith's concert.

    (D) A picture of Elliott Smith.

( ) 3. Which of the following statements is true?

    (A) Simon calls Blue when he finds out Blue's number.

    (B) Simon knows who Blue is all along.

    (C) Simon waits for Blue on the Ferris wheel.

    (D) Simon can't believe Bram is Blue at first.

1. In the email, what does Simon say to/about Blue? Why do you think Simon says so?

   _____

   _____

   _____

   _____

   _____

   _____

2. Why do you think Simon decides not to call Blue directly after getting his number? What is the significance of the note?

   _____

   _____

   _____

   _____

   _____

   _____

3. In chapter 32, we finally know who Blue really is. What does his decision to show up say about him?

   _____

   _____

   _____

   _____

   _____

   _____

Confess Your Love

In chapter 31, Simon finally plucks up the courage to confess his love for Blue. Please recall what other characters do to confess their love with textual evidence, whether it's love between siblings, friends, or couples.

Love between . . .	What do they do?
Simon and Blue	Simon writes a touching email that shows how well he understands Blue and how much he likes him. (p. 258)

Chapters 33-34
Pages 271-289

Word Power

1. attuned *adj.* 敏感的
2. materialize *v.* 突然出現
3. muster *v.* 鼓起 (勇氣)
4. meticulously *adv.* 嚴謹地

5. tongue-tied *adj.* 說不出話的
6. luminous *adj.* 發亮的
7. accost *v.* 走近談話
8. deliriously *adv.* 亢奮地

Reading Comprehension

( ) 1. Which of the following statements is **NOT** true?
   (A) Blue and Simon sneak out for lunch together.
   (B) Blue and Simon have the same English class.
   (C) Simon is quite satisfied with Blue's music taste.
   (D) Simon gets tongue-tied when speaking to Blue.

( ) 2. What do Simon and Bram do on Facebook?
   (A) They post a picture of themselves.
   (B) They change their relationship status.
   (C) They share their favorite songs.
   (D) They leave comments on each other's posts.

( ) 3. What does Martin say in his email?
   (A) He says he is homophobic.
   (B) He says he is in love with Simon.
   (C) He says he deleted the post on his own.
   (D) He says his family is conservative.

Further Discussion

1. What is the significance of Simon and Bram changing their relationship status?

_____

_____

_____

_____

_____

_____

2. What do you think about Martin at the beginning of the novel and then after reading his apology email? Do you see any change in him?

_____

_____

_____

_____

_____

_____

3. What do Simon and Leah talk about in Leah's car? Why does Simon cry after their conversation?

_____

_____

_____

_____

_____

_____

Apology Letter

As a result of Leah and Simon's conversation in the car, they finally get to fix their relationship. Try to sort out the thoughts and feelings they have shared. Imagine you were Simon, and apologize to Leah in the form of a written letter.

Chapter 35
Pages 290–303

Word Power

1. dim *v.* 使變暗
2. navel *n.* 肚臍
3. raptly *adv.* 全神貫注地
4. synchronicity *n.* 同步
5. gobsmacked *adj.* 瞠目結舌的
6. orchestrate *v.* 精心策畫
7. beeline *n.* 直奔
8. gush *v.* 誇張地稱讚

Reading Comprehension

( ) 1. What does Abby do on the talent show?
    (A) She dances solo while a violinist is playing.
    (B) She plays the violin alone on the stage.
    (C) She sings several pop songs by Adele.
    (D) She dances in perfect synchronicity with her group.

( ) 2. What is Simon's reaction when seeing Nora's performance on stage?
    (A) He is pissed-off to see her on stage.
    (B) He is disappointed at her performance.
    (C) He is sad that Nora never told him about her performance.
    (D) He is proud of Nora.

( ) 3. Why does Alice suggest Simon and Bram use the magic words?
    (A) So that they can join the trip to The Varsity.
    (B) So that they can pass the final examination.
    (C) So that they can have two hours at home unsupervised.
    (D) So that they can get two Frosted Oranges for free.

1. What is Simon's reaction when seeing Nora on the stage? Why does he feel this way?

   _____

   _____

   _____

   _____

   _____

   _____

2. On page 293, Simon mentions what Bram told him: people really are like houses with vast rooms and tiny windows. What is your interpretation of Bram's words?

   _____

   _____

   _____

   _____

   _____

   _____

3. What does Simon think when he concludes that his mom is about to have a big discussion with him?

   _____

   _____

   _____

   _____

   _____

   _____

Book Critic

Congratulations on finishing *Love, Simon*. Now imagine you are a renowned book critic, and your fans are waiting for your review of this book.

My Rating:

1. Introduce the book. What are the themes of this book?

   _____

   _____

   _____

   _____

   _____

2. Share your favorite part of the novel.

   _____

   _____

   _____

   _____

   _____

3. Give a recommendation. (E.g. if you like . . ., you will love this book or I recommend this book to anyone who likes . . . .)

   _____

   _____

   _____

   _____

   _____

◆ Wonder 解讀攻略

戴逸群 編著／Joseph E. Schier 審閱

Lexile 藍思分級：790

☞ 議題：品德教育、生命教育、家庭教育、閱讀素養

◆ Harry Potter and the Sorcerer's Stone 解讀攻略

戴逸群 主編／簡嘉妤 編著／Ian Fletcher 審閱

Lexile 藍思分級：880

☞ 議題：品德教育、家庭教育、多元文化、閱讀素養

◆ Matilda 解讀攻略

戴逸群 主編／林佳紋 編著／Joseph E. Schier 審閱

Lexile 藍思分級：840

☞ 議題：性別平等、人權教育、家庭教育、閱讀素養

Answer Key

Lesson 1

Reading Comprehension
1. (D)   2. (C)   3. (D)

Further Discussion
Question 3: L stands for Lesbian; G stands for Gay; B stands for Bisexual; T stands for Transgender; Q stands for Queer. Simon identifies himself as gay.

Lesson 2

Reading Comprehension
1. (D)   2. (A)   3. (C)

Lesson 3

Reading Comprehension
1. (B)   2. (C)   3. (D)

Read Between the Lines
Garrett, Abby, Nick / Leah, Simon, Blue

Lesson 4

Reading Comprehension
1. (D)   2. (D)   3. (C)

Lesson 5

Reading Comprehension
1. (A)   2. (B)   3. (C)

Lesson 6

Reading Comprehension
1. (C)   2. (A)   3. (B)

Lesson 7

Reading Comprehension
1. (B)   2. (D)   3. (A)

Lesson 8

Reading Comprehension
1. (C)   2. (C)   3. (D)

Lesson 9

Reading Comprehension
1. (C)   2. (A)   3. (B)

Lesson 10

Reading Comprehension
1. (A)   2. (D)   3. (B)

Lesson 11

Reading Comprehension
1. (C)   2. (B)   3. (A)

Lesson 12

Reading Comprehension
1. (B)   2. (B)   3. (D)

Lesson 13

Reading Comprehension
1. (A)   2. (C)   3. (B)

Lesson 14

Reading Comprehension
1. (D)   2. (B)   3. (C)

Lesson 15

Reading Comprehension
1. (B)   2. (C)   3. (C)

Lesson 16

Reading Comprehension
1. (C)   2. (A)   3. (D)

Lesson 17

Reading Comprehension
1. (D)   2. (B)   3. (C)

Lesson 18

Reading Comprehension
1. (A)   2. (D)   3. (C)